HUMANITY LOST

Meghan Douglass

Copyright © 2021 Meghan Douglass

All rights reserved

No part of this book may be reproduced, or stored in a retrieval system, or transmitted in any form or by any means, electronic, mechanical, photocopying, recording, or otherwise, without express written permission of the author.

The characters and events portrayed in this book are fictitious. Any similarity to real persons, living or dead, is coincidental and not intended by the author.

Cover design by: Michael Douglass
Edited by: Susan Setford

For my family who have supported the pursuit of my dreams (and nightmares).

CONTENTS

Title Page
Copyright
Dedication
Epigraph
1	1
2	19
3	29
4	33
5	41
6	59
Acknowledgement	61

What makes us so different,
What makes us still human,
If we succumb to devolution?

Running from home,
Seeking refuge in space,
Cannot change the fate of the human race.

Are we worth saving?
There's always a cost,
No hope... in the end, humanity lost.

S. MARGRET

1

The blaring alarms rang throughout the ship, loud enough to wake the dead. Six stasis pods opened simultaneously, the doors swinging outwards as their groggy occupants awoke, all feeling a little shell-shocked as well as freezing cold.

Gradually becoming more lucid, they all saw the menacing red light strobing from above their heads, filling the hibernation compartment with a demonic glow. The continual blasting scream of the alarm alerted them all to the fact that something was very wrong.

The Captain was the first to regain focus enough to step out of his pod, grab the robe hanging from the side and move. He needed to get where he could work out what was going on and somewhere he could warm up. He had no idea how long they had been asleep, but they weren't meant to have awoken until Earth was in sight again. Either way, he knew the siren and the red light meant something was not right.

He made it to the observation deck, its expanse of floor to ceiling windows normally warming but now uncharacteristically cold. Fear settled in. If this room was cold, it meant they were nowhere near any stars, which also meant they were nowhere near Earth.

The all too familiar pattern of his crewmates' footsteps from behind told him they had shaken off their grogginess and were on their way. He moved to a control panel and set to work as fast as he could.

The biting chill of the hull against his feet forced his first decision to turn up the heat in the room. None of them would think straight if they were shivering. Then he began to go through the information on the display, familiarising himself with their present status and why they had been prematurely aroused from their slumber.

The blue glow from the screen lent an eeriness to the distinct features of Captain Dahmer, highlighting his crooked nose and the streaks of grey in his hair which had first appeared halfway through their journey. It had been a stressful trip which had aged him considerably. The lines in his face had deepened and the bags under his eyes had become much more prominent.

He had been given the command of the massive cargo ship, the Valhalla, Earth's last hope. Leaving Earth, he had known it would be a do or die mission.

As the other crew members filed into the room, each face now almost as familiar to him as his own, he waited for one of them to point out the obvious. But he didn't have to wait long.

"Hey Captain, that doesn't look like Earth." After twelve months of Simmons' pathetic attempts at humour, the Captain was in no mood and glared back.

Simmons was a geologist, important for the mission but, in the Captain's opinion, very little else. Just looking at his goofy expression and thin, lanky body fed the exasperation which had been building inside him throughout their long journey. His whole appearance was almost comical, with his weirdly buggy eyes which were ever so slightly offset, but the Captain was far too irritated to laugh anymore.

Simmons had been an integral part of the overall success of their mission, but he had not been the first pick for the job. Coming second in most of the tests and not being the best match personality-wise, he wasn't a great fit. He was good, but not the best. The person originally picked for the mission had come down with a severe case of gastroenteritis the week before the crew were due to depart, a sudden and unfortunate turn of events. With them too weak to fly, the role had fallen to Simmons. He was no one's first choice, but in Simmons' eyes, second best was good enough.

Ignoring the comment with a dismissive wave of his hand, the Captain continued to look through the ship's log and navigation systems. He needed to assess their current situation and plan his next move as fast as possible.

By the time the Captain turned around to address his crew, the room had become warm enough for everyone to have stopped shaking and colour had returned to their cheeks, making them all look much more alive.

As all eyes turn to him, his appearance gave off a commanding air. His thick hair, made no less attractive by the grey peppered throughout, and thick muscles which were obvious even beneath the loose-fitting robe, projected the image required for a leader. His fitness, strength, and bravery were outdone only by his intelligence.

"You've probably all noticed that we're not anywhere near Earth and we won't know exactly where we are until we get to the bridge. What I can tell you is that we were woken up too soon when the ship detected a mechanical fault, but again I can't yet determine where it is or the extent of the damage until we get to the bridge. What I do know is that the oxygen systems are working fine, and the water recycling system is online and operational."

Audible sighs of relief rippled throughout the room at this information. He hadn't mentioned their food supply because he was hoping to have everyone back in stasis within a few days and so it wouldn't be an issue. For now, his focus was on the immediate problems at hand.

His crew were the best and brightest, well, almost all of them were, but they were all resourceful and multiskilled. Because of the minimal crew numbers allowed for this mission, they were all specialists in one area but trained in multiple others. This meant, in a pinch, they could pick up another person's duties to ensure the operation of the ship was maintained. So far, it hadn't come to that.

The crew all stared at the Captain, awaiting further orders.

"Everyone, get to your stations and give me a status update in fifteen minutes. We need to know how far we are from Earth and that the payload is safe. Without the payload, this entire mission will have been a waste."

With that, they all moved to leave the observation deck. While it may have sounded dramatic, it wasn't without truth. Every one of them knew all too well what it would mean for Earth if they didn't get the payload home.

The Captain lingered a moment longer, staring out into the vast expanse of space that lay before him. Their mission was to travel deep into space, further than anyone had travelled before, in search of new energy resources. Earth's reserves were nearing depletion and all nearby supplies within the solar system had been exhausted, forcing humankind to venture deeper out into the rest of the galaxy.

The Valhalla was designed and built solely to bring home the essential supplies required to ensure the survival of humanity. Its unique design meant it could safely store and transport the large amounts of fuel so desperately needed back on Earth while being manned with only a minimal crew.

The mission had been tough on the Captain and crew but, with the valuable resources they had secured, humanity now had a future. They had used the last of the fuel available on Earth for their journey. With what they found, they could now fuel the dozens of Generation Ships waiting back on Earth ready to seek new planets suitable for habitation. This mission was the last hope for humanity's survival.

The Captain made his way to the bridge, hoping everyone would have good news for him. He ran into Ramirez on the way, who reported no issues in the Medical Bay. He had expected none, but was glad of the news.

Ramirez was the ship's only doctor. While everyone had basic first aid training, he was the one they needed for any real medical emergencies. He'd been selected for the mission because his advanced surgical training was deemed essential in case of any accidents with the complicated mining equipment. Not only was he an accomplished physician, but he could also learn the basic training required much faster than all the other doctors in line for the position.

Although he was physically fit, his caramel-coloured skin was covered in a light sheen of sweat and his dark wavy hair had become pasted to his forehead. His run from the Med Bay after such a long time at rest had taken more out of him than he'd expected. He wrung his smooth, delicate surgeon's hands together as he kept pace with the Captain.

As the Captain stepped onto the bridge, Ramirez was still prattling in his ear explaining, in way too much detail, everything he'd checked. The Captain knew it was the stress making him talk too much, but it was already grating on his nerves as much as Simmons' lame jokes.

They had all spent too much time living in close quarters and longed to be back on Earth, living far apart from each other for a while—a long while. There had been more than one heated argument throughout the mission and many unpleasant words were thrown around. While they had attempted to match the crew based on personality, it had been more important for each to have the skills essential to make the mission a success, and so their personal comfort was really of secondary importance.

He turned away from Ramirez to talk to Jax, the ship's engineer, ignoring the grunt of protest behind him. Jax would have the information he really needed, which was what had happened to the stasis pods.

"Give me some good news Jax." She looked back at him, the deep concern she was trying to conceal being all too visible. A feeling of dread crept over him and a shiver ran down his spine. She was one of the strongest, most determined women he'd ever met and if she was even a bit concerned, things had to be very bad.

"Sorry Cap, it's not good. It looks like the ship was hit by a micro-meteorite, too small for the auto-navigation systems to pick up and alter course, but big enough to do a decent amount of damage to some of the ship's major systems. The hull has been punctured, but the ship sealed off that section automatically. I won't know the full extent of the damage and if I can repair it until I get outside but, based on what I'm seeing here, I'm not feeling optimistic."

She didn't sugarcoat it, which he appreciated. Of all his travel companions, she was the only one who hadn't aggravated him.

Jax had a good head on her shoulders. She knew when to talk and when to listen. He respected both her work and intelligence but, more than anything, her unwavering professionalism, which was something the others had allowed to lapse from time to time throughout their journey.

She'd already pulled her long brown hair into a tight ponytail, a habit which showed she was fully focussed and ready to get down to business, a small kink in the hair on the side of her head showing she'd done it in a hurry.

Jax had been carefully selected from a group of one hundred engineers for her ability to adapt, reinvent, and think on her feet. All invaluable skills on a mission where they could not carry spare parts for everything. Her diminutive figure disguised her physical strength, which had meant she'd spent a lot of her life being overlooked. But when it came down to it, she passed every test faster and more efficiently than anyone else there. This had won her a seat with the crew that was going to save the world.

"Thanks, Jax. Suit up and go check it out as soon as you can. Just make sure all other primary systems are up and running first."

"Already done, sir, and they all look good. There are a few secondary systems down, like the recreational holo-room, but nothing we desperately need."

Simmons muttered in the background, "Speak for yourself." The Captain shot him a glare and Simmons threw his lanky arms up in the air in a show of mock innocence.

"Report to me the second you're back onboard, Jax. Simmons, since you're always so eager to talk, tell me, is our payload safe?"

"Right you are, Cap'n," He fired back with an exaggerated salute. He could follow the orders given to him, but there was always an undertone of sarcasm and disrespect to everything he said. "The payload is safe and sound."

The relief the Captain felt at these words outweighed his continued exasperation with Simmons. The payload was safe. No matter what, they had to get it back to Earth. They were the last hope for humanity. No one would survive much longer the way things were. The mission came first. Everything else was secondary, and every member of the crew was acutely aware of this.

He walked over to his second in command, hoping to hear good news about their proximity to home. If they were only days away from Earth, things could still be OK. If they were further, then they would need those stasis chambers up and running again, and fast.

The ship was only equipped with enough food for the completion of the mission plus a small amount extra. They were never meant to be awake for any longer than was necessary so, to conserve energy and minimise weight, they had to limit certain supplies, food being one of them.

Cassidy's brow furrowed in deep concentration. She had a severe case of bed hair—a mass of dark, curly frizz, wild and untamed after her long slumber in the stasis pod. She hadn't had a chance to control it back into its usual neat state. As she focussed, she ran one hand through the frizzy mess but never quite to the ends as it became entangled in the knots, then she would absentmindedly shake her hand free. She was so engrossed in what she was doing the Captain gave her a moment before interrupting.

Like most of them, she was also driving him completely crazy. She was smart, but sometimes a little smarter than he would have liked. Deep down, he knew she was more intelligent than him. The hard part was, at some point, she had worked that out too. She said nothing out loud though and for that he was grateful.

Cassidy was the youngest Second-in-Command in history. She had passed all the tests as well as, if not better, than the Captain had, and the reason they had given him the top job over her came down to experience. He had fifteen years of experience on her and had even captained one of the last ships to leave Earth before the fuel situation had become so perilous. He was glad she was good enough to respect his experience and take orders along with the rest of the crew when required.

While she could frustrate him, she was nice to

look at. Her dark skin and even darker eyes always appeared so mysterious and alluring, yet also intimidating. She'd left a whole host of disappointed men back on Earth when she'd flown off to be a hero. But, as attractive as she was, it didn't take away from the fact that she could still piss him off.

Cassidy looked up from the screens in front of her. She understood the food situation just as well as the Captain and, from what she'd overheard, she knew there was no guarantee of the stasis chambers coming back online. She felt her stomach churn with anxiety as her mind whirred with mental calculations, finally ready to respond to the Captain's enquiry.

"It's not good, sir. We're at least two months from Earth, and that's our best-case scenario providing the damage to the ship isn't more severe than we think." The Captain's heart sank.

"Come with me Cassidy. We need to check the food supply and secure it before everyone else realises what's happening." He kept his voice low so he couldn't be overheard by the others working at their nearby stations.

They got up to go to the kitchen and heard a crunching sound from the corner of the bridge. Simmons was sitting there stuffing his face with an enormous bag of potato chips. The Captain stormed over and grabbed the bag out of his hands, walking away without a word with Cassidy following hot on his heels as Simmons' shouts of protest followed them out the door, crumbs flying from his mouth as he did so.

As they walked, he radioed Jax to get an update. The echoey sound that came back told him she was still in her extra vehicular activity suit outside the ship.

"How's it looking out there, Jax?"

"It's bad Captain. The external damage from the micro-meteorite was minor and I've patched the damage to the hull already. Once I get back inside and repressurise this section of the ship, I can check the extent of the internal damage. From what I could see, it doesn't look good. I'll see what's salvageable or if I can fix it with the supplies we have."

"Thanks, Jax. Report back when you can." The Captain signed off, his concern deepening.

He'd reached the kitchen with Cassidy, the motion sensor lights filling the room with a bright fluorescent glow as they entered. The giant pantry and cold room, which had stored all their food supplies, were both depressingly barren.

They had exhausted most of their supplies during the twelve-month mission. In hindsight, this might not have been their best move, but at the time it hadn't mattered. They had stuck to their daily rations for the most part and had only the occasional celebratory splurge. The biggest celebration was the day they had finished collecting their payload just before heading home.

It was an enormous party with Simmons even bringing out a bottle of Champagne he'd smuggled on board just for that occasion. It was against protocol to have alcohol on the ship, but the Captain let the contraband slide. They had all worked hard and deserved at least one night to relax and enjoy their triumph before they went into stasis.

They had piled up all the best snacks, cranked the music and enjoyed the tingling of the Champagne bubbles on their noses. While there wasn't enough for any of them to actually be drunk, the excitement and atmosphere of the evening had made them all feel giddy. It was the best night of the trip for everyone and one of the few times they all felt perfectly happy.

They scoured the corners of every cupboard, finding a couple more bags of potato chips, two tins of tuna, three tins of beans, a bag of flour and a dozen dehydrated meals. With six of them on board the ship, this would not last them long if they didn't start getting people back into stasis soon.

"We need to lock this up somewhere securely, sir. Then we can ration it out appropriately to last as long as possible. I think things are going to get a little hairy if Jax can't get the pods up and running."

The Captain knew she was right, so together they collected it all up and stashed it in the Captain's quarters, hidden and locked away. He sat down on his bed to consider their situation while Cassidy paced about the small room in front of him, deep in thought.

Priority number one had to be getting the ship safely back to Earth with the payload intact. The materials they had mined could fuel all the Generation

Ships that had been built, allowing people to leave the toxic planet and find more fuel and resources beyond the solar system.

They also had more information on several potentially habitable planets that the first ships could get to with relative ease. The world had become so reliant on technology for everything, including the generation of food and clean water, that without enough power to sustain everything, people were dying. The reliance on fossil fuels had lasted longer than anyone had expected and, as a result, Earth had become uninhabitable. Every house needed industrial strength air filters to manage the noxious air, and these all required power to run.

The radio buzzed in his ear and Jax's voice interrupted his thoughts. "I'm sorry Cap, it's bad. It's real bad. There's been a massive amount of damage. The impact of the micro-meteorite has destroyed considerable chunks of the computer systems and there is no way I have all the spare parts I need to fix it. Even if I did, it would take me weeks, possibly months, to repair."

He somehow kept his tone neutral and calm, while deep inside he was panicking. This was not good, and he hoped Cassidy was devising a more useful plan than anything he could come up with. With all her pacing, she would wear a hole in his rug any second now.

"Thanks, Jax. I'll call the rest of the crew together. Meet me and Cassidy in the dining room as soon as you can."

"Sure thing Cap." She wanted to say more, to ask more, but she knew she'd get all the answers soon enough. She wasn't entirely sure she wanted to hear them anyway.

He called each member of the crew and asked them to meet in the dining room. Winding their way through the corridors together, he talked through the finer details of their plan with Cassidy as they went.

The crew were some of the best Earth had, so they had more of an idea of what was happening than the Captain realised. Their training and logic meant they were all able to keep their heads and show very little of the trepidation simmering below the surface. Simmons, though, had started biting his nails again, something he hadn't done for years.

They were all assembled a short time later in the dining room. Someone had put out a jug of water and glasses on the table, a pleasant touch to what would be an unpleasant conversation. The Captain was scared so he knew his crew would be too, but he'd talked it all through with Cassidy and they knew what had to be done.

Sitting at the table, he looked around at his five crewmates who, in some ways, were more like family. An annoying family, but still a family. Simmons sat with his knee jiggling up and down as he continued to feast on his frayed fingertips. Even at a distance, the Captain could see small droplets of blood forming at the cuticles.

"We're in trouble. We're at least two months from

Earth and the stasis pods are unlikely to be operational any time soon." The Captain started, unable to make eye contact with any of them. He focused his attention on a droplet of condensation snaking its way down the side of the jug as he spoke.

A nervous murmur arose through the small group, and everyone had questions, but all of them were clever enough to know the most obvious answers, so the Captain continued.

"We have oxygen and plenty of water, as there was no damage to the recycling system. But as you know, our food supplies are low. We didn't plan for this eventuality. We took a risk, and it didn't pay off." The Captain stopped to allow everyone time to process this information before he went on.

"Cassidy and I have locked away all the food and, with the help of Ramirez, will do careful calculations on rations for everyone. I won't lie, it's going to be tight."

No one said a word. What could they say? They knew the Captain was right. They didn't like what he was saying, but that didn't change the situation. The crew were all trained for tough conditions and had all been picked for their ability to think logically and look at the bigger picture. The bigger picture here was saving everyone on Earth. They would all do what they had been trained to do to ensure the payload made its way safely home.

Cassidy pulled out the rest of the bag of chips the Captain had confiscated off Simmons earlier and divided the leftovers between everyone, except Simmons of course.

"Hey, not fair," Simmons whined, throwing his head back in exasperation. The Captain glared back at him and Cassidy rolled her eyes at the protests. "Fine then, permission to be dismissed, Sir?"

Ignoring his tone, the Captain gave a sharp nod in his direction. He wanted Simmons around about as much as Simmons wanted to be there. He knew the decision was fair, and he knew deep down that Simmons did too.

Simmons stalked out. If the Captain had turned to look, he would have had front row seats to a shot of Simmons' middle fingers aimed directly at his back. Thankfully for Simmons, he hadn't, and the rest of the crew were too busy talking amongst themselves and eating their handful of chips to notice.

With nothing more to discuss, the Captain dismissed everyone else. "Get as much sleep and rest as you can whenever you can. Burn as little energy as possible and be sure to report to Ramirez first thing in the morning for a full physical. Thank you, everyone. You're all dismissed."

Everyone cleared out of the room, leaving the Captain alone. He ran his hands through his thick peppery hair, then over his eyes. He didn't know how they were going to get through this, but he knew he'd have to work it out somehow. Feeling a slight pressure on his right shoulder, he turned around to see Jax standing silently behind him, looking troubled.

"Sir, I will do my best to get the stasis pods back

online as fast as I can." Her normally sky-blue eyes had become as dark as a stormy ocean, reflecting the emotional storm raging inside her over their current situation.

He smiled back at her. "I know you'll do what you can. Just let me know what you need or who you need, and you'll have it. We need those pods up and running. We have barely a week's worth of food."

He could tell she was holding something back, that she didn't want to be on her own and he didn't blame her. But he needed to keep order on the ship as best he could and that meant no favourites. Maybe when they got back to Earth they could spend more time together, without the prying eyes of rest of the crew constantly on them.

"Goodnight Jax, get some sleep. I need you working on those repairs first thing."

"Sure thing, sir."

He heard her words, but the pensive look on her face told him everything. She was going back to work because to be alone with her thoughts right now was just too much. There was no way she was going to sleep easily until she'd fixed the stasis pods. He admired her tenacity and wouldn't stop her. He wasn't likely to be getting much rest any time soon either.

2

Days passed with very little work for most, but a lot for Jax and Madden. Madden was the ship's head research officer with secondary skills in engineering, and he was doing his best to assist Jax with the stasis pod repairs.

A nerdy, unassuming young guy, Madden wasn't the fittest, but his skills in other areas outstripped most. He had read more widely and researched more things than almost anyone on Earth. His somewhat limp blond hair and large, round glasses had allowed him to hide in the background most of his life, despite how extraordinary he was. This permitted him to continue research in several areas of science unencumbered. His research, however, had been noticed by many. The advances he'd made, and the understanding he'd developed of what made a planet habitable and how it could easily be made so, were invaluable.

He hadn't competed for the position like the others. He'd been sought out and specifically selected. He could no longer hide in the background. Every person on this ship had become a household name the day they had left. There were even action figures made of them all.

Jax knew the ship better than anyone. She understood the inner workings of the Valhalla inside and out, but she was grateful to have an extra set of hands. While Madden didn't have the same knowledge of their vessel, he could take orders and follow them to the letter. With his research completed and his reports for Earth all tidied up, he was of most use with Jax.

Throughout their trip, Madden had identified half a dozen planets worth exploring as possible colonisation sites. He'd also collected extensive data from the planet from which they had mined most of their consignment. The information he was bringing back to Earth was almost as valuable to everyone back home as the payload itself.

Jax finally felt like they were making progress. She was repurposing motherboards and power sources from non-essential systems of the ship and rebuilding the computers that controlled the stasis pods. The pods themselves were intact and, while not a simple fix, she thought she'd be able to get them up and running within the next couple of weeks.

They had been rationing the food as strictly as possible but were running out fast. They found a few more items of food scattered around the ship, including some carefully hidden snacks in Simmons' room which he was loath to part with. At the end of the day though, it wouldn't be enough to sustain them until they got back to Earth.

While the ship's navigation systems were mostly

autonomous, following a programmed course, the ship could not land safely on Earth without someone in control. At least one person had to see the mission through, or it would all be a waste of the world's last fuel reserves. They had to ensure at least one person survived.

Being the ship's only physician meant Doctor Ramirez oversaw the calculations of everyone's daily rations based on their known basal metabolic rate and their current daily exertions. Because they had to make the food last as long as possible, he had to undercut everyone's needs in perfectly calculated ratios. This meant that on most days more than one member of the team ended up exhausted, hungry and irritable, Ramirez included.

On the sixth day after their premature wake-up, Simmons was attempting to assist Jax while Madden worked outside the ship. He was salvaging what he could from the components outside while ensuring that the integrity of the ship's hull was maintained.

Simmons had limited knowledge of engineering, but Jax had needed an extra set of hands. Simmons hoped that by helping, he might earn a slightly bigger ration at the end of the day. All of them were wearing monitors that were accurately calculating their exact active calories each day.

Jax was using a laser cutter to remove chunks of the ship that were now superfluous to their ability to get home. She was hoping to repurpose them to fix the control systems for the stasis pods. Simmons was supporting them and grabbing them as they came off. They were both exhausted and grumpy and were now working in silence after an exchange of several heated words and sarcastic comments.

Jax was tired of Simmons' attitude towards everything, and Simmons was just fed up with everything. This, combined with inattention caused by the lack of food and sleep on both sides, led to the next major accident of the mission.

There was a loud crack as the section of bulkhead Jax had been cutting through broke free far more suddenly than either party had expected. Simmons thought he was supporting it, but he'd underestimated the weight. It had been a much heavier section than the previous ones Jax had cut free, and he went down with a crash. Losing his grip, the chunk of metal landed hard on his leg. A terrible scream broke through the silence of the ship and those who heard it came running.

Jax, in shock, was standing there watching her shipmate writhing in agony with his leg pinned to the ground. Her bleary eyes shifted as thumping footsteps were added to the cacophony Simmons was making.

"It... it was an accident. I should have warned him how heavy it was," Jax stammered, her body shaking.

"Move Jax," Ramirez yelled, making sure he could be heard over the screams echoing off the ship's metallic walls.

He, not unkindly, pushed Jax to the side to tend to the first actual patient he'd had all trip. Until now, no one had even had so much as a cold, so it had only been routine and unexciting physicals. He looked at the foot protruding from under the large metal beam, twisted at an unnatural angle. As horrified as he was by the situation, he felt a surge of adrenaline at the thought of being able to use his training again.

They had to get Simmons to the Med Bay fast so Ramirez could assess the mangled limb closer. He directed Cassidy and the Captain to help him lift and shift the beam. Once free, the three of them scooped up the now silent Simmons and carried him as fast as they could without injuring him further.

Jax watched on in dumb silence from the floor where she sat shaking with her arms wrapped tightly around her knees. Rocking back and forth as she watched the unconscious Simmons being carried from the room, unaware of her own swaying, foetal position and the soft whimpering sounds escaping her lips.

In the Med Bay, things looked grim. Simmons, blacked-out from the pain, was losing blood fast from what used to be his knee. All that was left now below the thigh was the crushed remnants of a kneecap with the flesh turned to a bloody pulp.

Ramirez knew what he had to do. He had been trained for high-pressure situations and, although a little rusty, he knew how to think and work fast. He wouldn't be able to save the leg, so it had to be amputated.

He needed someone to assist with its removal. Because Cassidy had a small amount of medical training, he asked her to stay. The Captain was grateful, the sight of the tenderised remains which used to be Simmons' leg was making his almost empty stomach churn and he was glad to be excused.

With Cassidy's help, Ramirez gave Simmons a light anaesthetic. Considering he was already passed out, it didn't seem necessary to give him too much. The instruments required for the amputation were all laid out, looking oddly macabre in the Med Bay's glaring white light. The sharp scalpels glinting, the sight of the laser bone saw making Ramirez itch to cut. He felt calm with the instruments of his trade close at hand.

He sliced through the undamaged flesh just above the mangled portion of the limb until he hit bone. Then, using the laser bone saw he severed the leg, filling the room with the scent of burning flesh before carefully sewing up Simmons' newly formed stump and bandaging him good and tight.

He wrapped up the severed leg in plastic and placed it into a large chest freezer in the back corner of the Med Bay on top of several frozen samples they had collected for future analysis. It seemed more logical than having it rot in a medical waste bag, but a niggling feeling told him he was doing it for another reason entirely. He just wasn't ready yet to admit what that might be, even to himself.

Simmons stirred through the fog of anaesthetic. Ramirez knew he didn't want to have the conversation that was coming, but he had no choice. Making sure the morphine was flowing just enough so

Simmons was coherent but hopefully sufficient to soften the blow of the bad news, he explained what had happened in his best calm doctor's voice. He was hoping Simmons would be capable of taking the news well, even though his bedside manner was a little rustier than he wanted to admit.

"So, you're telling me all I need is an eye patch and I'll be the first pirate in space?" Simmons grimaced with pain.

Ramirez didn't laugh at Simmons' forced attempt at humour. He could see the joke was strained, but he allowed Simmons to cope the way he always had by joking around. Ramirez was relieved at how well it had all gone and breathed a heavy sigh of relief.

Leaving him to rest, Ramirez went to talk to the Captain. He'd been halfway through updating the Captain on the food supplies before the accident. They were getting dangerously low, and he knew that the more they stretched the rations the more accidents were likely to happen.

He found the Captain alone on the bridge staring out into the black and unforgiving expanse of space in front of them. He looked for patterns in the unfamiliar stars, attempting to reconnect with a home he yearned for, but the attempt was futile.

"I've amputated Simmons' leg, sir. He'll be fine after some rest and, once we get back to Earth, they can fit him with a prosthetic. He'll be out of action for a while but will be able to get around in the wheelchair." The Captain's face flooded with relief at the news that Simmons would be ok. He may not like

Simmons all that much, but he had hoped to make it back to Earth with all his crew members alive.

Ramirez continued, "If we don't get the stasis pods up and running soon, that will be the least of our worries. The food isn't stretching as far as I'd hoped. I'm keeping it as lean as possible, but if today proves anything, it's dangerous for people to work with so little sustenance."

"Once Jax calmed down, I got a progress report on the repairs," the Captain responded. "She still isn't certain she will be able to fix the pods, and today's incident will set things back. I'm going to need you to think harder, Doc, because I'm all out of ideas. If we don't get this payload back to Earth then everyone will die, not just us."

The image of Simmons' broken and mutilated leg floated back into the mind of Ramirez and his stomach lurched as he remembered the troubling feeling which had prompted him to use the freezer over the usual medical waste disposal. This was not something civilised people would normally consider, but logic told him, if they wanted to stay alive, there was no other option.

"Simmons' leg, sir," his voice dripping with revulsion at having to say the words out loud.

"I'm talking about the food now Doc, not Simmons' le..." He trailed off as his brain pieced it together. His face turned a visible shade of green, but like Ramirez, he realised they were out of options. The question was, would the rest of the crew see it that way? They were all trained to do whatever was necessary to get the payload back to Earth. "Doc, can you call everyone to the Med Bay for me? Let's just hope they can stomach the news."

As Ramirez called everyone to Simmons' bedside, he couldn't hide the look of trepidation, which told an already tired and concerned crew that things were going from bad to worse. They all stood around looking drained, dark rings circling their eyes.

Jax had only just stopped shaking, but she still looked fragile and wouldn't stand near Simmons. The guilt she felt over the accident was weighing heavily upon her and she looked everywhere except for the blanket concealing Simmons' lost appendage.

"Everyone, I'm going to cut to the chase. We don't have enough food to get us through until either Jax gets the stasis pods back up and running or we get back to Earth." The Captain half expected them to look surprised or upset, but no one did. They had all been expecting this. Even Simmons couldn't muster up a smart-ass comment.

He continued, "After talking things over with Ramirez, we have a solution to extend our food supply. But you won't like it. Under different circumstances, it would be unthinkable, but there is too much at stake for us to consider morals as a priority at this point. Just know that if we could find any other way, we would."

The Captain hesitated, unsure how to say what needed to be said. Thankfully, Ramirez broke the silence for him.

"I amputated Simmons' leg. It was beyond repair. I couldn't do anything save it." He took a deep breath. "We now have a large piece of... meat sitting in the freezer."

The horror and revulsion on everyone's face mirrored his own feelings, but he could see them all thinking and calculating. There were no immediate objections. After a moment, the calm was shattered by Simmons' retching and gagging.

"I... I can't eat my leg. There must be another way." He paused, turning his still groggy head to look at everyone. "You can't eat me!" The hysteria in Simmons' voice was rising and Cassidy put a gentle hand on his shoulder to help calm him down. "Are you sure there is nothing else we can do?" he cried.

Without waiting for the answer, Cassidy interjected, "How long can we make the leg last?"

The Captain appreciated how most of them were taking it. It was the beauty of working with a group of highly intelligent scientists. It meant they knew what they had to do. Ramirez went through his estimations, and they all knew it wouldn't be enough, but it would buy them some time.

That night, the smell of sizzling meat filled the kitchen for the first time since they had woken, and everyone's mouth watered. Every one of them felt an odd shift deep inside their souls. After tonight, they would all be changed in a way they could never explain to anyone back on Earth. Things that no person should ever consider doing had now become necessary, reasonable, and entirely justifiable.

3

Another week passed and they were officially out of food. Tensions were running high and Jax was struggling to think straight enough to work on the repairs. Madden tried his best to help but, with Jax being so unfocused and irritable, he just got in the way.

They would survive a little longer without food, but they couldn't function properly as a crew. The Captain was being tested to the limits of his patience and Ramirez had been having nightmares since the day of the amputation. Every time he woke up on his small foldout bed, drenched in sweat, his stomach would audibly growl and it would take him several minutes to calm his frantic breathing.

Ramirez knew what needed to be suggested and that he'd have to be the one to do it. His nightmares had told him what needed to be done, and he knew the mission was more important than his sanity. So, he sought out the Captain to tell him. He did not expect his latest brainwave to go down as well as the last.

He found the Captain and received exactly the reception he'd anticipated.

"How can you even suggest something like that?

What we did with Simmons' leg was one thing. An horrific thing, but justifiable under the circumstances. What you are suggesting now is the stuff of nightmares!"

"Yes Captain, my nightmares to be precise, but we have no choice," he answered matter-of-factly. "You know the ship needs to be manned to land safely on Earth, so at least one person needs to survive this insanity to do that. If Jax has the energy to fix the pods then we can all survive, but that won't happen if we don't make sacrifices."

The Captain couldn't hide his disgust. "You've thought this through and planned it all out?"

"Yes sir, I have."

"Oh my God, man! This is unthinkable! It's insane!" cried the Captain, tearing at his hair as he paced back and forth. "What you are suggesting… you're turning us into animals!"

"I'm sorry, sir, we don't have a choice. There is no other way."

"So, what's this grand plan of yours then?" asked the Captain, his red face inches from Ramirez and fists clenched at his sides, his short nails biting into the palms of his hands.

"Jax needs to stay fully mobile to do the repairs and I need to remain fully functional to perform the surgeries safely." He phrased this carefully and almost sheepishly, knowing it could be considered cowardly or self-serving, but he was the only one with the surgical skills to keep the food supply coming and keep everyone alive.

"How convenient," the Captain barked, failing to keep the sarcasm out of his voice, but acutely aware that all this talk of eating again was making his stomach rumble. He knew he had to say yes, and it horrified him. As awful as the situation was, the leg hadn't tasted as bad as he'd thought it would, and they were all so hungry after all. "So, who's first?"

"Simmons is still recovering, so either you, Cassidy or Madden. One leg each and then reassess the situation?" He said it as a question, but realistically, who could argue with his logic.

"I'll go first. It's going to be hard enough to convince any of the others to go along with this. I have to lead by example. Let's not tell everyone. Get what help you need for the surgery and let's just get this done." The Captain wondered if he'd be able to stomach eating himself better or worse than he had Simmons. Either way, he was about to find out.

"Thank you, sir. I'm sure they will all come around once they understand there is no other way. I'll grab Cassidy."

After Ramirez had talked it all through with Cassidy and calmed down her hysteria, she reluctantly agreed to assist with the surgery.

They all made it through calmer than they had expected under the circumstances. The surgery went smoothly, and the Captain was recovering before anyone even noticed the three of them were missing.

The smell of the freshly cooked meat wafting through the corridors of the ship once again drew everyone to the kitchen that night. With the hot food in front of them, it was much easier to convince them all it was for the greater good. Their mouths salivated and despite their objections, they couldn't help being distracted by the oddly intoxicating smell, given they hadn't eaten in almost two days.

That night, even after what they had just consumed, their mood was the best it had been in days. The horror of their actions had been pushed aside by how comfortable they all felt with a full stomach.

4

Life on the ship continued, with the initial displeasure of the new routine diminishing over the next few weeks. The amputees were able to leave the infirmary after a few days of recovery, but their movement was restricted at first by the single wheelchair on board. They took time learning to use the makeshift crutches Madden had engineered for them. The fact he didn't have Jax's level of engineering skill didn't mean he wasn't useful. He was a genius, after all.

They had full stomachs, which meant they were coping with their latest situation a lot better than Ramirez could have hoped, and they had all come to actually enjoy their hot meals together. They could put out of their minds what it was they were eating and be content with the fact they were no longer hungry.

Cassidy had an updated estimate on their travel time to Earth and it was still at least a month and a half away, at best. They had come too far now not to keep on surviving, but Simmons was not keen to lose another leg. None of them were and Ramirez knew the others were feeling hard done by because he and Jax had kept both of theirs, with good reason of course.

Jax was finally making progress on the pods. She was sure she'd have one functional soon so Ramirez couldn't interrupt her work. She needed to keep going. Any downtime for even minor surgery wasn't worth it.

Ramirez knew he'd have to share in the sacrifice the others had made without compromising his ability to perform any future surgeries. He could learn to stand and balance without his toes, so he hoped that would suffice, at least for now. It wasn't much, but it might get them through an extra day.

The others seemed somewhat satisfied by his offering, but for how long. They had all now developed a taste for flesh. It was no longer just for survival. Each one of them had begun to crave it more and more but, for now at least, they maintained a level of logic and order to their cannibalism. They were scientists, after all.

At dinner that night, as they chewed the disappointingly small portions of meat off Ramirez's bones, Jax announced she would be ready to test the first stasis pod in the morning. A cheer went up around the room and her hungry crewmates momentarily forgot Jax's fully intact body.

They stayed up late playing poker that night to see who would be the first to go back to sleep in a pod. Because every member of the crew was competitive, it made for a heated game. Jax had to sit out of the game, knowing she couldn't compete because she had to repair the rest of the stasis pods, but she enjoyed watching.

As the night wore on it came down to a playoff between Madden and Simmons. Madden had been fighting for top position all night, everyone suspecting that his genius level memory had enabled him to count the cards. But at the end of the night Simmons had won, with everyone certain he'd cheated.

Simmons was fed up with all of it and wanted to be back on Earth away from these people who just couldn't take a joke. He also wasn't a fan of the idea of losing any more limbs and, since he was next in line to go again, he felt no qualms about doing whatever it took to win. He was not the slightest bit perturbed that by cheating, he was stealing someone else's place.

They all slept peacefully that night for the first time since they had awoken. Things felt like they might be starting to turn around.

Simmons was ready to go bright and early the next morning. He watched Jax tinker with the stasis pod one last time and run some final checks, but he was ready and raring to go. The Captain gave the all-clear after reviewing the results Jax gave him, then it was showtime.

Simmons hopped in and gave his signature mock salute to everyone as Jax closed the pod door on him. For once in his life, he had no witty remark, he just wanted to be asleep again.

Anticipation buzzed throughout the room as everyone felt a desperate need for this to work. Not only was it one step closer to them all being able to go back into stasis and get home alive, but it was also one less mouth to feed.

She started up the system she'd cobbled together, and it buzzed to life. She gasped, realising she'd been holding her breath and could finally relax. It was working and Simmons would go off to sleep, leaving the whole place a little more peaceful. She wouldn't have to feel guilty every time she made eye contact with him over the dinner table, watching him pick at the fraying bandages wrapped around his stump.

A buzzing sound started up and Jax leapt to attention, checking the computers to make sure all the parameters were in range. It all looked OK, but the sound was getting louder, and the back of the pod had started producing a trail of noxious black smoke which was slowly filling the room. She tried shutting it down, but nothing would respond.

"Get the door open, something's wrong!" she yelled. Madden made to move forward just as it exploded, blowing everyone off their feet and leaving their ears ringing. Madden hit the wall off to the side and lay motionless. Unconscious but still breathing.

Everyone's attention quickly snapped into emergency disaster mode. Cassidy took off as fast as she could on her crutches to the bridge to check the explosion hadn't caused any damage to the ship's integrity. Ramirez waited until the smoke died down a little and rushed forward to see what had happened to Simmons.

Ramirez yanked hard at the still latched door of the pod, ignoring the searing pain from the heat of

Simmons' fiery tomb on his hands, which he would later regret. The whole thing was hot as hell. After a minute of ineffectual pulling, he let go, allowing himself a moment to watch blisters forming on his hands like painful bubbles, ready to pop with the slightest pressure.

He wiped the front of the pod with his sleeve to see what he could of Simmons' state and as he did, the charred and melted flesh hanging from Simmons' skull fell forward with a dull thud against the glass. His eyes had melted, leaving hollow sockets in the gaping, misshapen blob which only vaguely resembled a face.

This should have horrified Ramirez. In his gut, he knew it should have shaken him. It should make him want to run and scream, but the only thing he felt was hunger. A deep, demanding hunger. His mouth filled with saliva and his stomach groaned loudly. He wanted to hate his reaction, he wanted to mourn the loss of Simmons, but he just couldn't.

He went over to Jax. "We'll need equipment to break into the pod. The explosion has sealed the door shut tight, but Simmons is gone."

She went pale, but her reaction was also dulled by the realisation of what this might mean. They were all so hungry. How could she be faulted for thinking anything else?

Ramirez went to Madden next to check him over. His motionless body lay spread-eagle on the floor, the shattered lenses in his glasses sitting askew on his face, but he was still breathing. A large gash on the side of his head trickled a small stream of warm, sticky blood through his blond hair. Ramirez would use the wheelchair left by Simmons to get Madden to the Med Bay and assess him properly there.

As he walked past the Captain who was busy slaying any small flames with a fire extinguisher, he said, "We'll be eating tonight sir, and it comes pre-roasted." He thought Simmons would have appreciated the dark humour in the comment, but the Captain ignored it and continued smothering the fires.

Ramirez continued to chuckle to himself as he wheeled the unmoving figure of Madden through the halls to the Med Bay, eerily silent after the chaos he'd left behind only moments before. Ramirez took a minute to reflect on the current situation. At least there was one less mouth to feed now.

He hooked Madden up to the monitors and got an IV line into him to get some fluids flowing before he took a moment to assess the damage to his own hands. The large blisters that had formed had all burst in the process of moving Madden to the Med Bay, clear fluid now leaking from the painful sores. The adrenaline rush of it all had kept him from feeling too much pain, but in the silence of the Med Bay it was now excruciating.

He spent some time cleaning the burns and bandaging his hands up before giving himself a decent dose of morphine. Once the pain was under control and he was again thinking more clearly, he finished his assessment of the motionless form of Madden, being sure to take careful notes. Once completed, he headed off to the dining room to give his report to the rest of the crew.

That evening, they sat around at dinner, all still shaken by what had happened. What was even more awful was that Madden was now on life support. Ramirez had reported back to the rest of the crew that Madden's brain had swollen from the impact of being thrown against the hard, metallic wall and was now brain dead. There was nothing he could do for him.

Simmons' flesh had been charred badly by the time they got to him, which reduced how much was edible. They outwardly grieved his loss, but internally they were all grieving the loss of the food too. As disappointing as this was, the reality that they wouldn't be able to get the stasis pods working now was apparent. They would have to find a way to survive. At least with Simmons dead and Madden brain dead, they had two fewer mouths to feed.

With Madden on life support, Ramirez delicately proposed a slow harvest to keep everything as fresh as possible. All the major limbs could go first and then he could start carving off pieces of flesh, then organs. Since he was brain dead, he wouldn't feel a thing.

They all debated this for a while, none of them surprised by the suggestion but all still attempting to cling onto what little humanity they had left. This was a step beyond what their already questionable morality had allowed. Using Madden as a living meat farm should have felt beyond imaginable, but it just wasn't anymore.

They all agreed, this was the most sensible solution. They had a brief ceremony to farewell their fallen companion, saying goodbye to a young man with so much promise and who had spent most of his brief life invisible and yet now was helping to save the future of humanity.

Because of the lack of urgency, Ramirez could take his time without assistance while the others focused on making sure the ship got back to Earth as fast as possible. The explosion hadn't done any major damage, but there was plenty to fix and monitor to ensure the ship got home safely.

Ramirez began to make the first incision and Madden's body flinched. Checking the door to make sure no one was watching, he carefully increased the anaesthetic dose. It wouldn't do anyone any good if Madden woke up now.

5

They feasted for a few weeks, impressed with how far they could stretch the rations and discovering the distinctive flavours and textures of the different parts of the body. In the end, they harvested all the organs, freezing anything they couldn't use immediately to make it last.

They should be getting close to Earth soon, but the Captain still saw no recognisable signs of home. He spent hours staring into space on the observation deck, being of no use anywhere else most of the time. They were nearing the end of their food supply, so he sought out Cassidy to get an accurate update on the time left before they reached Earth.

"Cassidy, what's our current ETA for Earth?" The Captain's voice sounded measured, but his mind was already a whir with what would happen if they were further away than expected.

"I'm sorry, Captain, but in the past three days the computer's calculations haven't changed even though we have been moving. I need to do a full reboot and get Jax to check the system for me. I'm sure we are still on track, which means we should be only a couple of weeks away now."

They would find a way to get through this, after

all, Jax didn't need both her legs now. A drop of saliva escaped the Captain's mouth and Cassidy saw it shining in the corner. She knew exactly what he was thinking because the rumbling in her stomach meant she was thinking the same thing. Jax was so young and pretty. Cassidy was sure she would taste the sweetest of all of them.

Jax assisted with the computer repairs and then reported to the Med Bay for her amputation. She should have felt something about the loss of her leg, but all she felt was an odd, sick curiosity deep inside, so much like Cassidy's. So far, the Captain had been her favourite, but she hadn't had a really good taste of Ramirez yet. She felt a strange, twisted excitement inside her at the prospect of finally tasting herself, unaware of the madness that was festering in her brain.

The weeks and weeks of only eating human flesh were beginning to change and warp them all. They were forgetting what normal food tasted like and worse still, they no longer cared.

The pain meds Ramirez gave her left Jax feeling euphoric as she ate her dinner that night. To her, it was the best meal she had ever had, and she looked hungrily at her other leg. It was just another excess appendage she could survive without, surely.

The next day, Cassidy ran the calculations over and over. She rechecked and rebooted everything a dozen times after Jax helped her fix the system, but she had no idea how this could have happened. They had travelled deeper into space than anyone ever had before according to her current calculations. The ship's guidance systems were supposed to be foolproof, and what she was seeing should have been impossible. They were not travelling closer to Earth at all. They were still in deep space. But where in deep space, she didn't know.

They were officially out of range of any star system recognisable to man, which meant they were no longer in their home galaxy. The inescapable fact was, they weren't just weeks from home after all. It meant they had no idea how far from the Earth they were anymore.

No matter how many ways she did the calculations, they all came out the same. Staring at the screen in front of her, she remembered her life back on Earth and all the things she'd left behind. Her loving family, all the adoring men that had given her so much attention, and her golden retriever, Trevor, who she would never see again. She felt a pang in her heart as she realised she would see none of them ever again. Even though she'd known it was a possibility when they had flown off, the reality hit her harder than she could ever have expected.

After everything they had done to keep themselves alive, they wouldn't be able to finish the mission. She was going to have to be the one to tell the others, but she didn't know how she could face them with such devastating news. She was struggling to come to terms with it herself, let alone say it out loud.

She chewed thoughtfully on the last of her Madden jerky, pondering for a split second about lying to everyone, but she knew it couldn't last. They would find out before too long and she'd have to explain why she had kept quiet. She felt her nerve begin to crumble.

They were Earth's last hope and yet they had no hope of making it home alive. She felt a deep sense of loss knowing the consequences of their failure, but the thought of telling the rest of the crew was so much worse, knowing she'd let them down too. They had eaten each other. She'd eaten herself, and for what?

She spat out the hunk of meat she'd been mindlessly chewing and wrote a quick note to the Captain before quietly winding her way through the ship's empty corridors toward the airlock. She didn't want to be a part of the insanity on board this ship anymore, and the loss she felt was a heavier weight than she could bear. To think of how logical all their choices had seemed, but she knew deep in her soul she could never continue to live with herself after the consumption of so much human flesh.

Sealing the door tight behind her, she felt a stray tear trickling down her cheek as she pressed the brief sequence of buttons to open the hatch. It flew open, releasing what was left of her body out into the endless expanse of space. A single tear froze in place, sparkling like a diamond beneath her now sightless eyes, as she was flung from the ship, her body drifting deeper and deeper into the unknown reaches of the infinite black void.

The Captain found Cassidy's note a short time later and the shock hit him like a ton of bricks. Not only was his second in command gone, but the discovery that they would never make it home now shook him to his core. If Cassidy's calculations were correct, they had failed. Not only would they die lost in the depths of space, but before too long, everyone on Earth would die too.

Jax and Ramirez walked onto the bridge, but the Captain stayed quiet for now about the situation. He had to tell them Cassidy was gone because they would work that out themselves, but he'd keep news of their proximity to Earth close to his chest for now. He would just explain she was struggling with life on the ship and the weeks of cannibalism, which was true, and just leave out the part about them never getting home.

He explained what had happened and how Cassidy could no longer live with what they had been doing. When he'd finished, he heard Ramirez curse from across the room, loud enough to draw the Captain's attention.

"How could she have been so selfish? To shoot herself out into space, leaving no body for us to eat!" The Captain understood what Ramirez was saying. What horrified him most was that Ramirez's anger actually made sense when it would normally seem warped and twisted. But he would never have said it out loud.

Ramirez's fury flowed off him in waves, his face a deep red of rage. He ranted and raved for the rest of the day, but the other two didn't feel the need to argue with him. They were both mourning the loss of a friend and a part of them understood the anger behind Ramirez's reaction, although not the extent of it.

Before dinner that night, Jax went to the observation deck to spend some time looking out into space. She wanted some time alone to say goodbye to Cassidy. None of them had stopped to properly say goodbye to the others, besides the quick ceremony they had held for Madden, and Jax wanted to take a moment to feel human again. To know she still had a semblance of her humanity left in her.

The Captain was sitting there alone with the lights off, the soft glow of a distant star creating a dull silhouette. Jax hesitated before moving to sit beside him, not wanting to be alone after all, and she hoped he wouldn't mind.

"Sir..." she faltered, not knowing what she really wanted to say. A stray hair from her ponytail fell across her eyes and she untied it, allowing the rest to fall around her shoulders. She started to gather it up again and changed her mind, pushing it behind her right ear instead and leaving the rest hanging.

"I'm glad you're here, Jax. I've just been thinking about how bloody awful things have turned out. I can't believe Cassidy killed herself." The mournful look on his face and the slump in his shoulders said more of the grief he was suffering than any words could.

"We're in trouble, aren't we, sir?"

"It definitely looks that way." He paused, trying to assess if now was a good time to drop the bombshell on Jax. "It looks like we aren't getting home... ever."

"Are... are you sure? I mean, we've been on track until now. How could that have changed?"

"I don't know but Cassidy found out and that's why she killed herself."

"Oh." Jax had no words. Her body shook with silent sobs of anguish for the enormity of her loss. Sorrow for the loss of their friends. Misery for the loss of their home and their failure to save everyone on Earth. Most of all, complete devastation for the loss of their humanity.

The Captain put his arm soothingly around her and she leant into his embrace. It wasn't a soft embrace because his once hard and toned muscles had wasted away from weeks of limited rations, but it was warm and the comfort it gave her was immense. They sat in silence for the rest of the night, both ignoring Ramirez's cheerful calls for dinner. Neither had an appetite and they were taking what little solace they could from each other.

They fell asleep in each other's arms on the observation deck, the vast expanse of space laying before them in all directions and not a drop of hope of home ever being within their reach again.

At some point in the night, Ramirez wandered past the open door of the observation deck and paused to stare at his final two companions embracing on the ground, sound asleep and holding each other as though they were the last two left alive. He felt a momentary stab of jealousy at the sight and headed back to the kitchen to find his own comfort in the left-over Jax roast he'd cooked earlier that evening.

As he chewed the tender meat, his brown eyes glimmered with dawning realisation he no longer needed physical human contact to feel connected to other people. He wandered through the ship for a while, listening to the hollow sounds of his footfalls bouncing off the metallic walls around him, before heading to his quarters and laying down for a deep, peaceful sleep.

The Captain and Jax woke up in the morning early, both stiff and a little sore from sleeping on the cold, hard deck plates. They tried to shake off their embarrassment at having spent the night together while quickly straightening up their clothes.

"I'm sorry sir, I was just upset last night. I'll get back to work." Jax hurried out of the room on her crutches before the Captain could respond. He wanted to tell her he'd needed it more than she could ever know, but she was already out of the room.

They both returned to their small living quarters, freshened up and then went straight to work, carefully avoiding each other and Ramirez, along with the ghoulish breakfast that awaited them. Neither could stomach any more of what was left of Jax's leg. They would rather be hungry at this point.

Jax had gone back to tinkering mindlessly with the stasis pods, knowing she had no chance of fixing them in time but not letting that stop her. It kept her occupied, made her feel useful and gave her a moment to remember who she used to be and forget all the horrors threatening to overwhelm her.

Her thoughts drifted to the Captain as she worked away. He was handsome and the fact he was old enough to be her father didn't matter to her. His kind, rugged face floated into her mind as she remembered how safe she'd felt nestled against his strong, if slightly lean, frame.

She reached for her spanner absent-mindedly, not noticing it was resting against an exposed, live wire. Her fingers curled around the metal and a bolt of electricity shot through her body, twisting and warping it momentarily at an unnatural angle. The power in all nearby systems shorted and her limp body dropped the spanner. Soft tendrils of smoke rose lazily from what now looked to be the peacefully sleeping form of Jax.

The doctor was on the scene in seconds with his torch already in hand and his stethoscope draped conveniently around his neck. He shone the beam of light toward the exposed wires, checking that the spanner lying next to Jax's outstretched hand was no longer a danger.

He moved over to the fallen body, checking for a pulse and listening for a heartbeat, but Jax was dead. The electricity, which had jolted through her system with the violence of a lightning bolt, had stopped her heart instantly. It had been a quick and almost painless death. Ramirez smiled.

The Captain came at a run and stopped dead

when he saw what had happened. This was officially too much for him to handle. Jax was gone. The only one who had never caused him a moment of stress was gone and all because of a freak accident. As he stood there processing the scene before him, he realised there had been a lot of accidents since they had been woken up from their stasis pods. Their trip now felt truly cursed. This combined with the fact they were never getting home, made him feel like his mind might snap at any moment.

He looked over at Ramirez and caught the tail end of his grin. This made his stomach churn, and he shook his head, convinced he must have been mistaken. There is no way Ramirez would smile at a scene like this. There were only the two of them left now and there was nothing to be happy about.

"Captain, can you get the wheelchair so we can get her to the infirmary? I'll get what I can straight into the freezer," Ramirez spoke, without a hint of distress in his voice.

This routine had become far too second nature for him and, unable to ignore his part in all the madness, the Captain felt deeply disturbed. This, combined with the odd smile he was trying desperately to forget he'd seen, made him begin to question everything. It was taking all his energy just to keep his mind from fracturing and following Cassidy out of the airlock.

The Captain took one last look at the scene before him, absorbing the horror of it all. One final glance at Jax's limp body and the nearby exposed wires lit eerily in the narrow beams of light from their torches. Then he walked away. The lingering smell of death, which would never leave his nostrils again, followed him as he left. He locked himself in his quarters and decided to read over Cassidy's notes again to distract himself from the numb feeling growing inside of him.

There was nothing left to do, nothing he could do. He started going through the computer to work out how they had miscalculated so badly. They had thought they were on their way home. If they had made it, they would have returned as heroes, and no one would have questioned what they had done to survive because it would have saved the entire human race. And now it was all for nothing.

He searched all day and all night, ignoring Ramirez's knocks on his door, calling him for meals. Refusing to allow himself to eat any more of his crew members, he couldn't believe how far it had all gone. He felt intense grief at the loss of Jax. Deep down, he'd cared about her more than he'd realised. He'd never once taken the time to tell her how amazing she was. Even knowing Ramirez was out there munching on her fresh flesh made his skin crawl.

As he trawled back through the weeks of log entries, he found a glitch, a small bug in the system which somehow completely altered their tracking system. It was only noticeable because one day they were on track and the next they were in a completely unknown area of space. He remembered how Cassidy had to restart the system because it had stopped updating their position. He looked hard at the point in time the change had happened and saw the tiny anomaly.

Looking at the records, he could see only one person had logged on in between those times, and it was the ship's doctor. While not entirely unusual, as all crew members understood the flight and guidance systems in the ship, it was still a little strange. Considering Cassidy was in charge of getting them home and had been signed in only minutes earlier, there had been no need for Ramirez to even be looking at it, let alone changing anything.

Nothing was adding up. It took a bit of work, but he was able to remove the bug from the system. Then, he did a full reboot and recalculation of their position, and it now looked like they were only a week and a half from home. He sat staring at the screen in front of him in astonishment. They weren't the absurdly large distance from home Cassidy had gone to her grave believing.

This was incredible news. They could complete their mission after all, but Cassidy had thrown herself from the ship for no reason. Knowing Cassidy's need for perfection and her fierce determination to always be right and always be the best, he could have easily predicted her reaction to her discovery. They had spent so much time in such close quarters with each other, any of them could easily anticipate another's reactions.

The Captain felt a nagging itch of suspicion creep through him. Things did not feel right. So many accidents and mistakes. The image of the spanner lying next to Jax's hand and the exposed wire which had been the death of her. He struggled to believe that, even in her exhausted state, she would leave any live wires exposed and unprotected.

He thought back further to the day of the explosion and the loss of two of his men in one go. The explosion had happened because of a system malfunction. It was a mistake Jax hadn't predicted with the stasis pod she had patched up, causing it to overload. The door had sealed shut too tight to get Simmons out in time to save him from his fiery tomb. Ramirez had even been burned badly trying to get him out.

Madden, on the other hand, made less sense. He'd been thrown backwards when the system had blown. All of them were knocked off their feet in the blast, but he'd taken the brunt of it. His head had hit the wall hard, but had it really been hard enough to render him brain dead as Ramirez had told them? He had wondered, but he didn't think he'd ever know for sure.

The smell of cooking flesh wafted through the air vents, the Captain's traitorous mouth salivated. Instead of heading to the kitchen, he ran to his small sink and began heaving and heaving until his empty stomach hurt.

He'd followed Ramirez's lead on everything. After all, he was the ship's doctor in charge of the health and wellbeing of all the crew. It had all made sense. What other choice had they had? But he'd eaten people, his people. The crew he'd been entrusted to command. People he deep down cared a lot about and, in Jax's case, people he loved. How was he supposed to live with that?

Another knock sounded on his door. He had questions he desperately needed answered. It was time to face Ramirez, tell him the good news about home and ask a few questions about some of his suspicions.

"I'll be there in five," he called out, listening to the soft footsteps of a man he'd thought he knew and trusted, moving away from the door.

He splashed water on his face to clear his tired mind. The lack of sleep and immense grief was taking its toll. He wanted his brain to be sharp to face the coming conversation. He walked down the corridor trying to work out the best way to approach the situation, barely noticing the direction he headed. The ship had been his home for so long now he could have navigated it with his eyes closed.

Walking into the kitchen, he was met with the unfortunately intoxicating aroma of roasted flesh, which reminded him of how long it had been since he had last eaten. As much as his brain detested the idea of eating any more human flesh, his stomach betrayed him with its growling eagerness.

He sat down, deciding that if he ate, he'd have a clearer head and maybe he could get some of the answers he needed during the idle dinner chit chat. He watched Ramirez devouring his dinner like an animal, a look of sheer pleasure on his face as he focused on each tender mouthful. The Captain looked away, unable to watch the scene. It was almost as though he was intruding on a deeply sensual and private moment. Thankfully, the smooth jazz music Ramirez had put on for background noise was drowning out the sounds issuing from his mouth while being mildly disturbing at the same time.

The Captain was the first to break the silence. "So, I rechecked the ship's tracking and guidance systems," the Captain paused, noticing a slight shift in Ramirez's countenance. This told him everything he needed to know. "Looks like we're on track to get back to Earth after all. We'll be there in less than two weeks, and we should have enough food now to survive the rest of the trip."

Ramirez remained silent. He'd stopped chewing the tender roast cheek he'd been relishing, his hands shuffling restlessly beneath the table.

"I know you played a part in all this, but I don't understand exactly what or why. Hopefully, there's a reasonable explanation for what you were doing on the system between Cassidy's checks before she died. I'm hoping the bug I discovered wasn't put there by you."

Ramirez forced a grin, "Of course not Captain. I don't even know what you're talking about, but this is fantastic news. We'll be home soon. Our mission will be a success after all." They were both silent again, the distrust and tension palpable.

"I'll have to add this to my report and when we get back to Earth, there will be a full investigation into the entire trip. There has to be and I'm not sure how either of us will justify eating half the crew."

"Oh Captain," Ramirez sneered. "You won't have to worry about any of that, I promise."

He leapt from the table, the sharp blade of a kitchen knife glinting in his hand and he launched himself towards the Captain. The Captain was still fit, his reflexes were good and he moved fast, but not quite fast enough. He was well practiced on the crutches, but he only had one good leg, while Ramirez still had both of his.

As Ramirez leapt at him, he felt the knife pierce his arm and the muscle beneath the blade tear as Ramirez wrenched it free. The Captain roared in pain and tore away on his crutches as Ramirez righted himself. Ramirez paused to lick the warm, slick blood off the blade before he pursued his prey. The Captain couldn't get far.

The trail of thick red blood led him straight to the Captain's quarters and he typed in the override key on the door lock. They gave the doctor of the ship override codes to all rooms in case of a medical emergency. As the door slid open, he could hear the Captain recording a log with more information than Ramirez was prepared for anyone on Earth to find out.

"I think that's enough, sir." Ramirez's voice sounded both calm and terrifying. The Captain turned to face him, wincing with pain as he moved.

"You killed Cassidy. You killed Jax. Did you kill Madden too, and Simmons?"

"Hah! Simmons was all on Jax and deep down she

knew it too. Madden, well, he wasn't as brain dead as I may have told everyone he was, but he was far more useful to us dead than alive. I would never have had to kill Jax if that bitch Cassidy hadn't thrown herself into space. I liked Jax, but I like life more. We needed food, so they had to go." He inched closer as he spoke, his face dark and manic. "Deep down Captain, you know it was all for the greater good."

"You'll never get away with this!" The Captain's cliché line just made Ramirez laugh.

Ramirez leapt across the room. With his wound bleeding profusely, the Captain was unable to move out of the path of the knife fast enough and it landed square between his shoulder blades, piercing through to his rapidly beating heart. Blood poured from his mouth and onto the ground as he fell. The choking, gagging sound as his body gasped for air filled the room as he drowned in his own blood.

The mess would take Ramirez a significant amount of time to clean up, but at least he had plenty of food to keep him going. He could face any amount of work now until he was safely back on Earth, hailed a hero for saving humanity.

He spent the weeks to come feasting on the last of Jax and the Captain while ensuring all traces of their cannibalistic exploits were purged from the ship. It would do no one on Earth any good to find out what had gone down, and he wasn't going to risk tarnishing his record.

He shot any leftover remains into space. His plan was to explain to everyone that when the stasis pods had malfunctioned, one of them had exploded with Simmons inside and he couldn't be saved. He hadn't been able to scrape all the charred remains out of the pod, so he felt this was a plausible explanation. The rest of his remains were shot into space as an appropriate memorial for his service to the mission.

When the rest had woken, there had been a limited food supply left on the ship. There was only enough to sustain one person on the trip back to Earth. Knowing the ship only needed one individual to get it home safely, they had drawn straws for who would stay. The rest of the crew had bravely sacrificed themselves, shooting themselves out of the airlock into space so Ramirez could make it back home and save the planet.

He was almost grateful to Cassidy, her foolishness now leant a modicum of truth to his story, giving it a legitimacy it may not have otherwise had. He had been careful to alter all records of any persons on the ship from the time the pods malfunctioned. It had taken a lot of double-checking, but he was pretty sure he'd pulled it off.

6

The ship made a shaky but safe landing back on Earth. Although he was trained in basic flight and landing, Ramirez wasn't the most experienced pilot around.

The reception he received was beyond a hero's welcome. They hailed him as a God amongst men. The press conferences and the people crowding him day after day only served to feed his growing ego. The intoxicating number of choices surrounding him, so many delicious looking people. He was everyone's hero, and everyone wanted to be as close to him as possible. An endless supply of food at his beck and call. He'd never have to visit a grocery store again.

With enough fuel now, the Generation Ships began to leave Earth for brighter futures. Ramirez was one of the first to leave, as a reward for his services to humanity. An entire ship full of people, a proverbial smorgasbord for the man who now only had a taste for human flesh. If he was smart, and he was pretty sure he was smarter than everyone else now, he could keep it up forever.

The loss of his own humanity in the process of saving the rest of humanity was of no concern to him at all. Now he'd lost his mind...

ACKNOWLEDGEMENT

A huge thank you to both Michael Douglass and Susan Setford for their help and support with editing and giving me the time to make this book possible.

Printed in Great Britain
by Amazon